# Isabel's Favorite Things

# The Sound of Short I

by Joanne Meier and Cecilia Minden · illustrated by Bob Ostrom

**The Child's World**

Published by The Child's World®
1980 Lookout Drive
Mankato, MN 56003-1705
800-599-READ
www.childsworld.com

The Child's World®: Mary Berendes, Publishing Director
The Design Lab: Design and page production

Library of Congress Cataloging-in-Publication Data
Meier, Joanne D.
  Isabel's favorite things : the sound of short i /
by Joanne Meier and Cecilia Minden ; illustrated
by Bob Ostrom.
     p. cm.
  ISBN 978-1-60253-404-9 (library bound : alk. paper)
  1. English language—Vowels—Juvenile literature.
  2. English language—Phonetics—Juvenile literature
  3.  Reading—Phonetic method—Juvenile literature.
  I. Minden, Cecilia. II. Ostrom, Bob. III. Title.
  PE1157.M546 2010
  [E]—dc22                          2010002918

Printed in the United States of America in Mankato, MN.
July 2010
F11538

## NOTE TO PARENTS AND EDUCATORS:

The Child's World® has created this series with the goal of exposing children to engaging stories and illustrations that assist in phonics development. The books in the series will help children learn the relationships between the letters of written language and the individual sounds of spoken language. This contact helps children learn to use these relationships to read and write words.

The books in this series follow a similar format. An introductory page, to be read by an adult, introduces the child to the phonics feature, or sound, that will be highlighted in the book. Read this page to the child, stressing the phonic feature. Help the student learn how to form the sound with her mouth. The story and engaging illustrations follow the introduction. At the end of the story, word lists categorize the feature words into their phonic elements.

Each book in this series has been carefully written to meet specific readability requirements. Close attention has been paid to elements such as word count, sentence length, and vocabulary. Readability formulas measure the ease with which the text can be read and understood. Each book in this series has been analyzed using the Spache readability formula.

Reading research suggests that systematic phonics instruction can greatly improve students' word recognition, spelling, and comprehension skills. This series assists in the teaching of phonics by providing students with important opportunities to apply their knowledge of phonics as they read words, sentences, and text.

**The letter i makes two sounds.**

The long sound of **i** sounds like **i** as in: *bike* and *ripe.*

The short sound of **i** sounds like **i** as in: *itch* and *ditch.*

In this book, you will read words that have the short **i** sound as in: *six, fish, pig,* and *trip.*

Isabel is six years old. Her family is planning a trip.

They are going on a big ship.

"What can we bring on the ship?" asks Isabel.

"Can we bring our kitten?" asks Isabel.

"No, the kitten might get sick," says Mother.

"Can I bring my toy pig?" asks Isabel.

"No, it is too big to fit," says Mother.

"What can we do on the ship?" asks Isabel.

"We can watch the big fish swim," says Mother.

"We can skip on the deck.

Be careful not to trip!"

says Mother.

"We can sit on the deck.

The sun will feel good!"

says Mother.

"We will have a great trip!"
says Isabel.

# Fun Facts

Most pigs are big, but the largest was an animal named Big Bill, who weighed in at 2,552 pounds (1,158 kilograms)! Scientists consider pigs to be fairly intelligent animals and believe they are even better at learning tricks than most dogs. Many pigs live on farms, but people often keep potbellied pigs as pets. Perhaps you've heard of guinea pigs. These furry pets aren't pigs at all—they're rodents! People believe they may originally have been called pigs because they make noises similar to the squeal of a pig.

Maybe you've taken a trip on an airplane or even on a cruise ship. How would you like to go for a trip on a hot air balloon? In 1999, Bertrand Piccard and Brian Jones traveled around the world in a hot air balloon. The trip took them 20 days.

# Activity

### Planning a Trip with Your Family

It's fun to visit places far away from home, but you don't always have to get on a plane or drive far in the car to plan a fun trip! Talk to your parents about organizing a trip to the zoo or a nearby museum. If you live near a wilderness area, consider planning a hiking trip through the woods.

# To Learn More

**Books**
**About the Sound of Short I**
Moncure, Jane Belk. *My "i" Sound Box®*. Mankato, MN: The Child's World, 2009.

**About Fish**
Lundblad, Kristina, and Bobbie Kalman. *Animals Called Fish*. New York: Crabtree Publishing, 2005.
Sill, Cathryn P., and John Sill (illustrator). *About Fish: A Guide For Children*. Atlanta, GA: Peachtree, 2005.

**About Pigs**
Gibbons, Gail. *Pigs*. New York: Holiday House, 2000.
Older, Jules, and Lyn Severance (illustrator). *Pig*. Watertown, MA: Charlesbridge, 2004.

**About Trips**
Danziger, Paula, and Tony Ross (illustrator). *What a Trip, Amber Brown*. New York: Puffin Books, 2001.
Evans, Lezlie, and Kay Chorao. *The Bunnies' Trip*. New York: Hyperion Books for Children, 2008.

**Web Sites**
**Visit our home page for lots of links about the Sound of Short I:**
*childsworld.com/links*

Note to Parents, Teachers, and Librarians: We routinely check our Web links to make sure they're safe, active sites—so encourage your readers to check them out!

# Short I
# Feature Words

## Proper Names
Isabel

## Feature Words in
## Initial Position
is                    it

## Feature Words in
## Medial Position
big                   sick
fit                   sit
kitten                six
pig

## Feature Words with
## Blends and Digraphs
fish                  swim
ship                  trip
skip

## About the Authors

Joanne Meier, PhD, has worked as an elementary school teacher, university professor, and researcher. She earned her BA in early childhood education from the University of South Carolina, and her MEd and PhD in education from the University of Virginia. She currently works as a literacy consultant for schools and private organizations. Joanne lives in Virginia with her husband Eric, daughters Kella and Erin, two cats, and a gerbil.

Cecilia Minden, PhD, is the former director of the Language and Literacy Program at the Harvard Graduate School of Education. She is now a reading consultant for school and library publications. She earned her PhD in reading education from the University of Virginia. Cecilia and her husband, Dave Cupp, live outside Chapel Hill, North Carolina. They enjoy sharing their love of reading with their grandchildren, Chelsea and Qadir.

## About the Illustrator

Bob Ostrom has been illustrating children's books for nearly twenty years. A graduate of the New England School of Art & Design at Suffolk University, Bob has worked for such companies as Disney, Nickelodeon, and Cartoon Network. He lives in North Carolina with his wife Melissa and three children, Will, Charlie, and Mae.